I HERO

Gorgon's Cave

Steve Barlow and Steve Skidmore

Illustrated by Sonia Leong

W

FRANKLIN WATTS

LONDON•SYDNEY

First published in 2007
by Franklin Watts

Franklin Watts
338 Euston Road
London NW1 3BH

Franklin Watts Australia
Level 17/207 Kent Street
Sydney, NSW 2000

A CIP catalogue record for this book
is available from the British Library.

ISBN: 978 0 7496 7666 7

1 3 5 7 9 10 8 6 4 2

Printed in Great Britain

Franklin Watts is a division of Hachette Children's Books,
an Hachette Livre UK company.

Decide your own destiny...

This book is not like others you may have read. *You* are the hero of this adventure. It is up to you to make decisions that will affect how the adventure unfolds.

Each section of this book is numbered. At the end of most sections, you will have to make a choice. The choice you make will take you to a different section of the book.

Some of your choices will help you to complete the adventure successfully. But choose carefully, some of your decisions could be fatal!

If you fail, then start the adventure again and learn from your mistake.

If you choose correctly you will succeed in your adventure.

Don't be a zero, be a hero!

You live in the world of Ancient Greece, in the time of legend. The time of Heracles, Theseus and Jason; of Pegasus, the Minotaur and the quest for the Golden Fleece.

You are an adventurer. You have fought and won many battles against both warriors and monsters.

Now, you have been summoned by the King of the City of Thebes. Many years ago, the hero Perseus killed Medusa the gorgon. But now, Medusa's cave is once again haunted: by Medusa's sister, the gorgon Euryale; and the monster Typhon.

Like her sister, Euryale has snakes instead of hair. Her gaze is so terrible that anyone who looks her in the eyes will die. The monster Typhon is a snake below the waist, and has snakes instead of fingers.

You make your way to the royal palace to find out what the King of Thebes has in store for you.

Now turn to section 1.

1

The King looks tired and worried but his voice is firm.

"Typhon and Euryale have kidnapped Princess Theia, my only daughter," he tells you. "In daylight, they lurk in the Gorgon's Cave, far below the earth. But at night, they come out to plague the countryside, killing and eating men, women and children.

"Many heroes have set off to destroy the monsters. None have returned. You are my last hope. Will you go into the Gorgon's Cave, slay the monsters and rescue my daughter?"

If you say no, turn to 22.
If you say yes, turn to 35.

2

The monster charges as you draw your sword. You lash out at Typhon, but he is quick and clever.

His hands reach for you. Each finger-end is a snake's head, its fangs dripping with deadly venom. One scratch will be enough to kill you. You know you will not be able to dodge or shield yourself from them for long.

If you decide to attack Typhon's body, go to 40.

If you decide to attack Typhon's arms, go to 27.

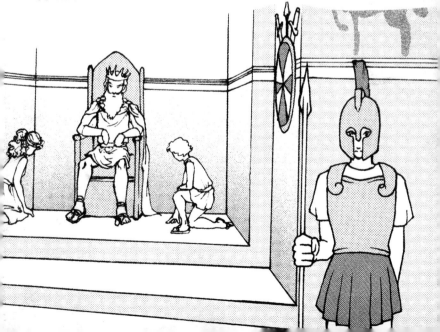

3

You empty the bag of food you have brought for your journey and fill it with gold and jewels.

But as you turn to leave the cave, a horde of terrible flying creatures appears. They have bat wings, the heads of dogs and snakes for hair. They are the Furies, and they carry whips to punish thieves and murderers.

They swarm around you. "Greedy fool!" they cry. "How will the treasure help you rescue the princess?"

They lash at you with their dreadful whips until the pain overwhelms you.

Your greed has been your undoing. You are no hero. If you wish to begin again, turn to 1.

4

You drop your spear and shield, and hack at Theia's chains with your sword.

But then you hear a hissing sound behind you. The princess screams and shuts her eyes. "Euryale!" she cries. "The gorgon is here!"

You spin around and raise your sword.

Go to 34.

5

As you make your way down the passage, you hear a moaning sound ahead of you. You move forward carefully and find a wounded man wearing the armour of a Greek warrior.

"I came here to rescue the princess," he tells you, "but I was attacked by Cerberus. I managed to get away from him, but not without terrible injuries. When I got to this point I found that I was too weak to go on. Please help me."

If you decide to help the warrior, go to 19.

If you decide your quest is too urgent to be delayed, go to 49.

6

You shake your head. "I will go to rescue the princess, but I don't believe in fortune-telling and prophecy. Besides, it is too far to go to the Oracle. If I am to help the princess, I must begin my journey at once."

You know that there is said to be a way into the Gorgon's Cave at the Pass of Athos in the North.

Go to 28.

7

The monster throws back its ass's head and laughs. "Mercy, mortal?" it brays. "The great Typhon knows no mercy!"

The snake-coils close tighter around you. You gasp for breath. Your ears ring, and darkness takes you.

Your adventure has ended. If you wish to begin again, turn back to 1.

8

You light your torch and find your way into the cave by the light of its flickering flame.

You travel through dark tunnels filled with the sounds of dripping water and the shrieks and howls of unknown creatures.

Your torch burns down and begins to sputter. Just as it goes out, you spot a side passage lit by a strange orange glow. You go through it and find yourself inside a chamber lit by a fire that burns from a crack in the rock. On a stone table you find a golden harp, a bronze helmet and a polished silver shield. They are clearly magical objects. You wonder if they are cursed.

If you decide to take them, go to 25.
If you decide to leave them, go to 42.

9

Watching Euryale's every move in your shield, you throw your spear. But Euryale dodges. Your spear misses its target and clatters harmlessly away into the darkness.

Euryale slithers towards you, hissing in triumph.

If you want to try your sword against her, go to 23.

If you decide to climb out of her reach, go to 18.

10

You puzzle over the message until you realise that the letters are in normal writing, but backwards. Using your shield as a mirror, you are able to read the message.

HE WHO WOULD FIND HIS WAY THROUGH THE LABYRINTH MUST TAKE THE FIRST TURN ON HIS LEFT HAND, THEN THE SECOND ON HIS RIGHT UNTIL HE COMES TO THE END OF THE MAZE.

You smile – you know what to do.

Go to 24.

11

You hack at the monster's snake fingers. You chop off several snake-heads, which fall to the floor still snapping and writhing. But with his other hand Typhon snatches your sword from you.

If you decide to turn and run, go to 33.
If you decide to throw your spear, go to 21.

12

The fight is short and brutal. Snarling like a demon, your foe tears at you with fearsome jaws. You fall to the floor, screaming, and the creature's teeth, sharp as daggers, meet in your throat.

Your adventure has ended. If you wish to begin again, turn back to 1.

13

The Oracle nods her head. "You have chosen wisely," she says. "Your errand is urgent. I shall summon Pegasus to carry you to Tenarus."

Go to 17.

14

You can see Euryale reflected in the polished metal of your shield, but the monster's hideous gaze has no effect on you. Euryale's snake hair writhes and hisses as she realises that her deadly power has failed.

She has lost the advantage of surprise and does not want to fight. She slithers back into a cleft in the rocks to hide.

If you decide to lure her out into the open, go to 31.

If you decide to follow her, go to 34.

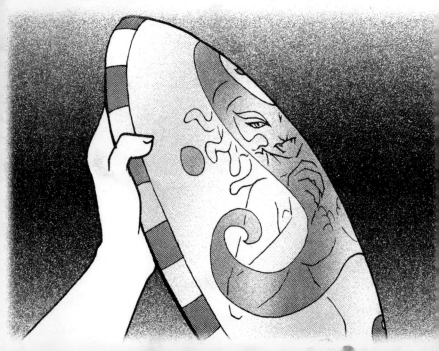

15

You come to a place where the stone tunnel you are following divides many times. You realise that you are entering a labyrinth – an underground maze.

If you want to take the next right-hand tunnel, go to 5.

If you want to take the next left-hand tunnel, go to 38.

16

You put to sea, but a terrible storm arises. The waves are whipped up into mountains of water that threaten to swamp the ship. Thunder roars overhead. In a lightning flash, you see jagged rocks jutting from the sea straight ahead. The captain tries to steer away from them, but it is too late. The ship is wrecked. You and the surviving sailors are cast up on an unknown shore.

Go to 39.

17

The Oracle leads you to a nearby hill top. Soon you hear the beat of great wings. Pegasus, the winged horse, arrives.

You pick up your oil torch, a flask of water and a bag of food for your journey. You take your sword and spear and leap up on Pegasus. Together you fly south. The air rushes by as you pass over mountains, and then across a sea dotted with islands.

You arrive at the base of a jagged mountain. You dismount, and pat Pegasus's neck. "Thank you, my friend," you say. Pegasus neighs and flies away.

You step into a narrow gorge at the foot of mount Tenarus. As you go forward, the way becomes gloomy and forbidding. You have reached the entrance to the Gorgon's Cave. You hear strange noises from within – tortured screams, cries of despair and mad laughter that makes your blood run cold.

If you are determined to enter the cave, go to 8.

If you decide to go back, go to 39.

18

As you climb the rough cavern wall, you see a crack in the rocks above you. A shaft of sunlight shines through it.

Euryale mocks you. "Yes, coward! That is your escape. Leave the princess and save your own skin!"

If you want to escape, go to 39.

If you decide to fight on, go to 20.

19

You give the warrior a drink from your water flask.

"Thank you, friend," he gasps. "You must leave me now, for I feel the hand of death upon me. But listen, before I came to these terrible dark paths, a wise man told me how to find my way out of the labyrinth. Always take the first passageway to your left, then the second to your right, and you will escape unharmed."

The wounded man's eyes close and his head falls back. He does not speak again.

You leave him and go on.

Go to 24.

20

You laugh. "I am no coward, Euryale. Surrender to me, if you want to live!" Euryale hisses with rage and begins to climb after you.

You climb onto a ledge where a huge boulder lies balanced on the edge of the drop. You brace your back against the cave wall and push at the boulder with your feet. Your muscles are on fire. Sweat pours from you. Your heart is pounding. You are about to give up when the boulder begins to move. You push even harder. The boulder rolls over the edge with a grinding of tortured rock. Too late, Euryale realises her peril. The boulder topples onto her and the monster is crushed.

Go to 50.

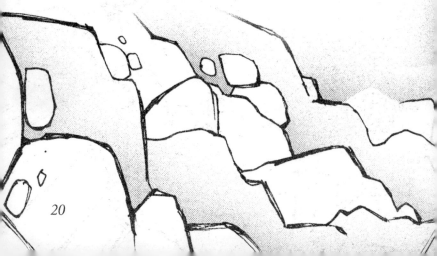

21

You know you will only get one throw of your spear to defeat the monster. You dodge its lunges, looking for an opening. At last, you have a clear throw.

You hurl your spear right into the monster's left eye. Typhon gives a terrible scream of rage and pain. Then, with a crash that shakes the whole cave and brings stalactites raining down from the roof, he falls to the floor, dead.

Go to 26.

22

"Your daughter is beyond help," you tell the King. "This is a mission for a fool, not a hero."

You leave the palace. But an old blind man stops you in the street. He grips your arm and says, "He who refuses to help a child in need is no hero."

"How do you know what I have just done?" you ask.

"The blind know things that are hidden from those who can see," replies the old man.

You are ashamed and ask the old man what you should do.

"Go to the Oracle. She will help you find your way."

If you decide to go to the Oracle, go to 44.

If you decide to ignore the old man's advice, go to 6.

23

You lunge at Euryale with your sword.

The monster's tail sweeps round and knocks you across the cavern, slamming you into the hard stone wall. Now you are weaponless.

If you want to fight Euryale with your bare hands, go to 41.

If you want to climb beyond her reach, go to 18.

24

You pass through the labyrinth unharmed. At its end you find two doors guarded by living skeletons. Above the doors are written the words:

ONE DOOR LEADS OUT
OF THE LABYRINTH.
THE OTHER DOOR LEADS
TO DEATH.

YOU MAY ASK THE GUARDIANS
ONLY THREE QUESTIONS.
ONE GUARDIAN TELLS ONLY LIES,
THE OTHER TELLS ONLY THE TRUTH.

CHOOSE YOUR QUESTIONS
WISELY, TRAVELLER.

You ask the guardian of the left-hand door which is the way out. He points to the door he is guarding and says, "This way."

You ask the guardian of the right-hand door which is the way out. He points to the door he is guarding and says, "This way."

You have used two of your three questions and you are no wiser.

If you decide to take the left-hand door, go to 30.

If you decide to take the right-hand door, go to 49.

If you decide to think further about the problem before choosing, go to 43.

25

You put on the helmet and take the harp and the shield. As you leave the chamber, you realise that now you are wearing the helmet, you can see in the darkness without a torch.

But as you turn a corner, you are stopped in your tracks by a blood-curdling growl. Crouched in front of you is a fearsome, three headed dog! It is Cerberus, dreadful guardian of the underworld!

You have heard that the singer Orpheus once sent Cerberus to sleep by playing his harp: but will it work for you?

If you decide to play the harp, go to 37.
If you would rather fight Cerberus, go to 12.

26

Leaving the body of Typhon, you go on, still deeper into the cave.

Before long you find yourself in the biggest cavern you have ever seen. At the far end, chained to a pillar of rock, is a young girl – the Princess Theia. She is overjoyed to see you.

"I knew someone would come and rescue me!" she cries. "Please – let me out of these chains."

If you decide to release Theia immediately, go to 4.

If you decide to look around first, go to 47.

27

You lash at the monster's arms with your sword, but Typhon pulls them out of reach. Before you realise it, his snake-tail has coiled around you like the body of a python. The tail tightens around you. In your agony, you drop your sword, your spear and your shield. You cannot breathe. You are being squeezed to death.

If you decide to bite the monster, go to 36.

If you want to beg Typhon for mercy, go to 7.

28

You travel north on foot and arrive at a small fishing village. You persuade the captain of a trading ship to take you on the first stage of your journey by sea. However, on the day you are to set sail, the weather is bad. The old sailors sitting on the harbour wall shake their heads in warning.

"A storm is coming," one tells you, "a bad one. You had better not put to sea until it passes."

If you decide to ignore the old sailor and set sail, go to 16.

If you decide to listen to his advice and wait, go to 48.

29

You arrive at a cave full of treasure. Gold, diamonds and other precious jewels litter the floor of the cave and are piled high in its centre.

If you decide to take as much of the treasure as you can carry, turn to 3.

If you decide to leave the treasure and go on, turn to 15.

30

On the other side of the door, the tunnel becomes wider. There are no more side passages! You have escaped the labyrinth – but your quest is not over yet.

Go to 45.

31

You turn to look back the way you have come.

"Oh, no!" you cry. "The monster Typhon is coming! I am no match for him and Euryale together."

Euryale does not know that you have already killed Typhon. She thinks that he is on his way to help her, and comes out of her hiding place.

If you want to hurl your spear at her, go to 9.

If you want to lunge at her with your sword, go to 23.

32

You lie on the furs and doze off.

Then, suddenly, you are wide awake. Someone is singing. A young woman enters the chamber. Her face is like a mask and her eyes are blank and empty. You try to get up, but something in her song has made you as weak as the harp made Cerberus. You cannot move a muscle.

You realise with horror that the young woman is a lamia – a terrible bloodsucking vampire – and you are her helpless victim.

Your adventure has ended. If you wish to begin again, turn back to 1.

33

You dodge between stalagmites, trying desperately to escape. But the snake-tailed monster knows the cavern and is faster over this rough ground than you are. As you race towards the exit, you stumble and fall. The last things you see are the poisonous snake-fingers of Typhon reaching out to draw you into his deadly grasp.

Your adventure has ended. If you wish to begin again, turn back to 1.

34

You look straight into the eyes of the gorgon.

Euryale's gaze is deadly. You are instantly paralysed, unable to move. You feel numbness spreading inwards from your feet and hands. Soon, every part of you will be turned to stone, even your heart.

You have become another stone statue in Euryale's collection. If you wish to begin the adventure again, turn back to 1.

35

The King is delighted. "I know you have the courage for the task," he tells you. "Yet against Euryale and Typhon, courage will not be enough. You should go to the Oracle. She will be able to tell you how to defeat the gorgon."

If you take the King's advice and go to the Oracle, go to 44.

If you decide to ignore the advice, go to 6.

36

You lower your head and bite hard into the monster's tail. You choke on the creature's blood and its flesh tastes disgusting, but you know you cannot afford to let go. You sink your teeth deeper.

The monster roars and uncoils. You tear yourself from its clutches and pick up your sword and spear.

If you want to continue to fight with your sword, go to 11.

If you decide to throw your spear, go to 21.

37

As you run your fingers over the strings of the harp, you find that the magical instrument is playing itself. Cerberus becomes sleepy. His growls die away. One by one his three heads droop. The great hound lies sprawled on the floor of the cave, snoring.

You lay the harp, still playing, beside the sleeping monster's head. Carefully, you make your way past Cerberus and go on down the tunnel.

Before long, the way divides.

If you want to take the passage leading upwards, go to 46.

If you want to take the passage leading downwards, go to 29.

38

You find a chamber with a strange message carved in the rock:

> HE WHO WOULD FIND HIS
> WAY THROUGH THE LABYRINTH
> MUST TAKE THE FIRST TURN
> ON HIS LEFT HAND, THEN THE
> SECOND ON HIS RIGHT UNTIL HE
> COMES TO THE END OF THE MAZE.

You scratch your head. Someone has gone to a lot of trouble to carve this message into the rock, but you can't read a word of it.

If you decide that the message is nonsense and you should ignore it, go to 49.

If you decide to try and decipher the message, go to 10.

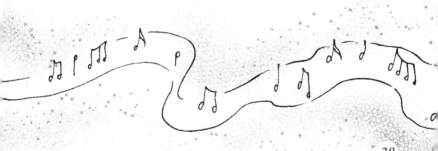

38

39

You decide that anything is better than continuing with this nightmare quest. You leave the scene of your failure. You struggle back to Thebes over mountains and deserts. You are forced to sell your weapons and armour to buy food.

By the time you reach the city, you are little more than a walking skeleton. The King sends you away. "You set out from here a warrior," he cries angrily, "but you return as a beggar. You have failed my daughter. You have failed me. You are no hero."

Your adventure has ended. If you wish to begin again, turn back to 1.

40

You lunge at the monster's chest with your sword. The blow strikes home – you have drawn first blood! But you have only scratched Typhon, and now he is angry. With a roar he reaches for you again, his snake fingers hissing and writhing.

If you want to continue to fight with your sword, go to 11.

If you decide to throw your spear, go to 21.

If you decide to turn and run, go to 33.

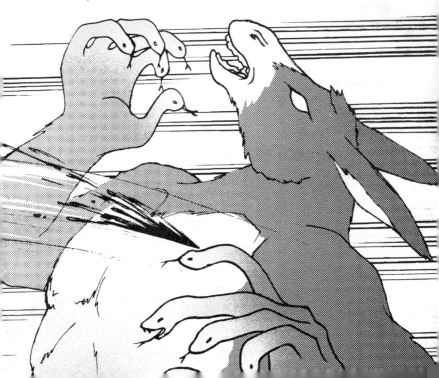

41

Euryale laughs. "Fool!" she cries. "Your puny human strength is no match for mine!"

She tears the shield from your grasp and forces your head round to meet her dreadful gaze.

Go to 34.

42

You leave the objects and return to the passage. Outside the chamber, you can see nothing without your torch. But you can hear the padding of gigantic feet – or paws – coming towards you. Some deadly creature is prowling the tunnel ahead of you.

If you decide to make your escape while you can, go to 39.

If you decide after all to return to the chamber for the helmet, harp and shield, go to 25.

If you decide to fight, go to 12.

43

After some thought, you believe you have solved the riddle of the doors.

You say to the guardian of the left-hand door, "If I asked the other guardian which door leads out of the labyrinth, what would he say?"

The guardian replies, "He would tell you that the right-hand door leads to the way out."

You continue. "If you are the guardian who tells only the truth, then the other guardian would be lying, and the right-hand door must lead to death.

"And if you are the guardian who tells only lies, then the other guardian would tell me that the left hand door leads to the way out, and he would be speaking the truth.

"Either way, the right-hand door leads to death and the left-hand door leads to the way out."

The guardians step aside and you go through the left-hand door.

Go to 30.

You visit the Oracle and ask her how you may succeed in your quest. The Oracle tells you that there are two ways to the Gorgon's Cave. One entrance is at the Gorge of Tenarus in the south, the other by the Pass of Athos in the North.

"Take the southern entrance," the Oracle tells you. "Nothing but disaster awaits you in the North."

If you decide to take the Oracle's advice and head south, go to 13.

If you decide to ignore the advice and head north, go to 28.

45

The tunnel widens further to become a great cavern with stalactites hanging from the roof and stalagmites growing from the floor.

A terrifying roar echoes through the cavern. You gasp and cover your ears.

In the centre of the cavern floor stands a huge creature with an ass's head, a man's body and the tail of a snake. It is the monster Typhon. It reaches for you, roaring, with its snake fingers coiling and hissing.

If you want to fight Typhon, go to 2.
If you decide to run, go to 33.

46

You come to another chamber. There is a stream flowing through it with a soothing ripple of water. A stone platform covered with furs offers a comfortable bed. It is a long time since you have slept and you are very tired.

If you decide to stay in the chamber and rest, turn to 32.

If you decide to leave the chamber and go on at once, turn to 15.

47

Ignoring the princess's pleas, you unsling your shield and strap it to your arm. You draw your sword. You look around the cavern, peering into the shadows.

You hear a hissing from a side chamber. Euryale is here! You prepare to do battle.

If you decide to meet Euryale face-to-face, go to 34.

If you decide to look at Euryale's reflection in your shield, go to 14.

48

Heeding the old sailor's advice, you wait for the storm to pass. But days later, the wind is still howling and the sea is still rough.

You decide that you can go no further without the Oracle's help and travel to see her. "I realise that I shall never reach the Gorgon's Cave by sea," you say. "Tell me what I should do."

"You must fly south on Pegasus, to Tenarus."

You bow your head. "Very well."

"Then my blessings will go with you."

Go to 17.

Knowing you cannot lose valuable time, you press on. But soon you become hopelessly lost in the maze of tunnels.

Suddenly, a flock of large, bat-like creatures flies down the passage towards you. They knock the bronze helmet from your head. Without it, you are suddenly blind. In the darkness, you stumble into a pitfall and plunge down a seemingly bottomless shaft into the bowels of the Earth and oblivion.

Your adventure has ended. If you wish to begin again, turn back to 1.

You release the princess. You help her to climb the wall of the cavern into daylight and find that Pegasus is waiting for you.

Together, you and Theia mount the winged horse and fly back to Thebes.

The people of the city are delighted by your safe return with their princess. They carry you in triumph to the palace, where the King and Queen promise you a rich reward.

You have completed your quest. You are a hero!

I HERO

If you enjoyed reading

Gorgon's Cave

there are more titles in the
I Hero series:

Viking Blood

978 0 7496 7665 0

Death or Glory!

978 0 7496 7664 3

Code Mission

978 0 7496 7667 4

Code Mission

Steve Barlow and Steve Skidmore

Illustrated by Sonia Leong

It is May 1944. You are an agent of the British Special Intelligence Service (SIS) – a top-secret unit. You speak several languages and are an expert in handling many types of weapon. During the course of the war against Nazi Germany, you have taken part in many successful operations behind enemy lines.

During the last six months, you have carried out several spy missions in northern France in preparation for the Allied invasion of mainland Europe. Now having completed your latest mission, you are back in London on leave.

However, your well-earned break is interrupted by a phone call from General Alan Cummings, the head of your section at SIS.

I HERO
DECIDE YOUR OWN DESTINY
Code Mission
Steve Barlow - Steve Skidmore